STO ✓

FRIENDS
OF ACPL

3 1833 04393 6795

W9-DFT-439

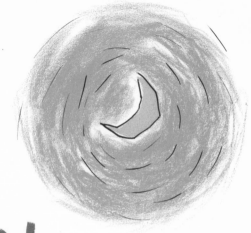

TAMARINDO!

by Marcia Brown

CHARLES SCRIBNER'S SONS NEW YORK

TO PEPINEDDU

Copyright © 1960 Marcia Brown

All rights reserved.

A—9.60 [JCJ]

PRINTED IN THE UNITED STATES OF AMERICA

Library of Congress Catalog Card Number 60-13486

CO. SCHOOLS C503177

One two one two...

Three little boys paraded up and down in the shadow in front of the church. Their general, Pepineddu, kept his eyes on them while he finished writing a letter for Aunt Nunzia. Then he ran to take command of his army.

Cosimo was the captain,
Pierino the lieutenant and
Tonino was the private.
His legs were very short.

Suddenly, into the square ran old Uncle Neddu. In his hand was a piece of frayed rope.

"My donkey! Tamarindo! He's gone!"

The little girls left the figs they were turning on the drying trays, old Marinetta left her bench in the sun, Rocco rushed out of his shop and led the old man over to a chair in front of the café. Pepineddu called, "Riposo!" At ease!

Everyone crowded around. A donkey lost! That was a serious matter! Even Tonino knew the importance of a donkey: to carry olives to the olive press, grapes to the wine press, beans to the house, faggots to the fire.

Uncle Neddu could not say much. He was in despair. "Tamarindo! He ran away in the night. He is young ... such a deep chest, legs like pillars. You can tell him by his ears ... straight up to hear which way the wind blows ..."

"He is young..." The people looked at each other and shook their heads. In the hot sun *who* could think of running after a young donkey with pillars for legs, and ideas of his own about how to spend a summer's night!

Pepineddu could. "Attenti!" He drew
up his men. "You Cosimo live on the hill and know
the path up through the olive trees. You Pierino
often go to the lemon groves with your father. And
you Tonino . . . well, you can come too."

Pepineddu added to himself, "And I know the
way over the cliff to the sea where the black cave
is." But he said nothing. A general does not like to
frighten his soldiers.

"We will find Tamarindo for you,
Uncle Neddu."

"Attenti! Avanti! March!" One two one two ... across the square they marched, through the narrow alley, toward the country. Now there were no more houses. "Riposo!" called Pepineddu, and the soldiers broke ranks.

First they went down through the
lemon trees, then over the stone walls
of the terraces and down through
the fig trees.

3 1833 04393 6795

Everywhere they saw leaves half
eaten. But they saw no young
donkey with his ears
straight up . . . only Uncle
Alfio's Pinotto, and he was
so old that his ears hung down
like banana leaves in the sun.

They crossed the
brook and climbed the
hill where the peach
trees grew.

They looked in
Uncle Tonio's
little house, but
found only
chickens.

Up the hill, past the cemetery, past the villa of Don Paolo, past the little farm of Uncle Alessio, who called to them from under his medlar tree. "Some donkey has trampled my new beans!"

Then up the hill and over the ridge the soldiers went, until they came to the smoky gray olive trees. They saw the bushes eaten, the fences tumbled, the farmers angry, the gardens trampled; but they saw no young donkey with his ears straight up.

They stopped to suck some prickly pears. It was then that they saw the white goats on the path that led down to the sea. Alfio the goatherd was not to be seen.

"Let's follow them!" Down the path the boys slithered and slipped, down the rocks to the sea. Then they remembered. "It's hot!"

Off came their clothes, and in they dove, Pepineddu first, Cosimo and Pierino after. Tonino followed the minnows close to shore.

When Pepineddu came up for air, he gave a shout. "The goats! They've stolen our clothes!"

For the little white goats had each taken a piece of clothing—just to taste, mind you. And off they went leaping over the rocks as if they had springs in their hooves. Out of the water and up the rocks the boys scrambled after them. Pepineddu tore after one white goat with a black eye. The goat had his shirt in his mouth! Suddenly the goat jumped. Before he knew what he was doing, Pepineddu jumped too—and found himself in the dark.

Pepineddu could not see a thing, but he heard a sound ahead of him.

"That goat's eating my shirt," he thought. Just then there was a roar that raised the hairs on his head. There in the dark shone two big eyes. Pepineddu backed up fast—

Too fast! He sat down hard.
Over him hung a dark muzzle and two big
ears—that stood straight up! Tamarindo!
"Eeeeeee AaaaaaaW!"

The others came running. "It's Tamarindo!" Sure enough, there was the other piece of frayed rope around his neck.

"EEEEEEEEEEE-AAAAAAAAAAWWW!"
Together they pushed and pulled the donkey out of the cave. The goats were forgotten.

"Up, everyone!" The boys leaped onto the donkey's back. Pepineddu, then Cosimo, then Pierino. Tonino rode in front of Pepineddu.

Up the path they went, past the smoky gray olive trees, down through the peach trees, over the brook, up through the fig trees, over the wall, up through

the lemon trees. Then down the little path and through the alley to the village square. The village was waking up after the siesta.

"Tamarindo! They've found Tamarindo!"
Triumphantly the four boys entered the square.
"We found him in the black cave by the sea!"
Marinetta stirred her bones and ran for a towel, Aunt
Nunzia whipped off her apron, Rocco brought a cloth,
and Uncle Neddu took out his large handkerchief.

Ecco! The soldiers were dressed.

"Marinetta, have you a piece of ribbon?" Marinetta found a piece left from the festa. "And scissors and pins?" Solemnly, Uncle Neddu cut the ribbon into four pieces. Then he pinned a piece on each soldier.

"For bravery and accomplishment," he said. "How can I thank you?"

CO. SCHOOLS C503177

"Like this," said Rocco, and he asked all four boys to sit with the *men* under the cool leaves of the pergola in front of the café and eat pomegranates and fresh, ripe figs. And how the men laughed to hear about the goats!

When Pepineddu went into the house he pinned the ribbon under the picture of Santa Rosalia on the wall.

A little later he heard the bell of Alfio the goatherd. Pepineddu ran out to get his milk. There was the white goat with the black eye.

"He's wearing my shirt!" Alfio grinned as he handed Pepineddu a bundle.

"Your uniforms, General," he said, and saluted.